# ALONE!

# PAVILION

For Mum and Dad, with love.

First published in the UK in 2021 by
Pavilion Books Company Limited
43 Great Ormond Street
London, WC1N 3HZ

Text and Illustrations © Barry Falls, 2021

The moral rights of the author and illustrator have been asserted.

Publisher: Neil Dunnicliffe
Editor: Hattie Grylls
Art Director: Anna Lubecka
Designer: Sarah Crookes

ISBN: 9781843654674

A CIP catalogue record for this book is available from the British Library.

10 9 8 7 6 5 4 3 2 1

Reproduction by Mission, Hong Kong
Printed by Toppan Leefung Printing, China

This book can be ordered online at www.pavilionbooks.com,
or try your local bookshop.

MIX
Paper from
responsible sources
FSC® C104723
FSC
www.fsc.org

# ALONE!

Find me in every picture!

# BARRY FALLS

There once was a boy called Billy McGill

who lived by himself…

...on the top of a hill.

He spent every day in his house all alone...

...for Billy McGill liked to be on his own.

"This is my hill," said Billy McGill.

"I live here alone!

Always have, always will."

Splendid alone-ness. Yes, that was the aim.
So nobody called and nobody came.

Life was so fast down below in the town
with the people, the traffic, the rushing around...
...the HUSTLE and BUSTLE, the coming and going,
the world never stopped with its

TOING-AND-FROING.

But life on the hill stayed
exactly the same.

Nobody called.

Nobody came.

"This is my hill,"
said Billy McGill.
"I live here alone!
Always have, always will."

From morning to night,
and all the year round,
there was barely a whisper,
and hardly a sound.

Not a PLIP!
Not a PLOP!
Not a HUM!
Not a CREAK!

'Til one day – the HORROR!
a
# SCRATCH!
and a
## SQUEAK!

Billy searched high and low
and ALL OVER the house,
until under the bed
he discovered…

…a MOUSE!

"No," Billy muttered.
"I can't accept that."

So he went to the town and he brought back a CAT.

"This is my hill," said Billy McGill.
"I live here alone! Always have, always will.

This cat will give chase to the mouse,
yes it will!

And then peace will return
to my house on the hill."

But the cat liked to play,
and the mouse was the same,

and they both thought
the chase was a
WONDERFUL
GAME.

"Oh no!" Billy cried,
"It's a dog that I need.
It'll chase off this cat
and this mouse
with great speed!"

But the dog joined the game
with the cat and the mouse,
and they ran round in circles
all over the house.

"Oh No!" Billy cried.

"What they need is a scare."

So he went to the zoo and snuck out with a BEAR!

But the bear, feeling tired,
collapsed in a heap,
with the cat and the mouse
and the dog, fast asleep.
"Oh no!" Billy cried.
"I must wake them up quick!"

"A ROAR from a TIGER
just might do the trick!"

But the tiger he fetched had a terrible SNEEZE
and the ROAR, when it came,
was no more than a WHEEZE.

"This won't do," Billy said. "I must fetch him a vet,
for I will get rid of these animals yet!"

"This is my hill," said Billy McGill.
"I live here ALONE!
Always have, always will."

The vet, when she came, said
"Let's knit him a sweater!
This beast has a cold,
it will make him feel better."

"I can do it for you, you must get me some wool.
Fetch a SHEEP with a coat that is fluffy and full."

So the sheep Billy found was

as BIG as a

CLOUD!

"How on earth
will I clip it?"
he wondered aloud.

"My friend's a hairdresser,
he'll know what to do,"
said the vet.
"He will shear this sheep
nicely for you."

So the vet asked her
friend "Can you help?"
He said "Maybe…
as long as you're
there to look after
my BABY."

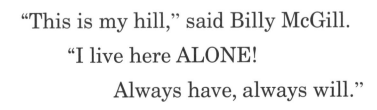

"This is my hill," said Billy McGill.
"I live here ALONE!
Always have, always will."

As soon as they came,
the poor babe started crying,
and the hairdresser said

"There's just
NO USE in trying!

I can't shear
the sheep while
my baby's upset!

We must get him a TOY,
oh the poor little pet!"

"To the TOYSHOP!" said Billy. "I'll be back very soon!"

He returned with a
fabulous, bright
red balloon.
"Oh, how perfectly
chosen!"
the hairdresser said.

"His favourite colour has
always been RED!"

But just at that moment
the wind began BLOWING...
the house was beset by a

# THUNDERSTORM

# GROWING!

The balloon disappeared
in a gust through the door.
The hairdresser SCREAMED!
The baby cried SORE!
"ENOUGH!" Billy roared,
"I can't take any more.
All this noise and confusion,
and what is it for?

THIS IS MY HILL,

I AM BILLY MCGILL.

I LIVE HERE ALONE!

ALWAYS HAVE,

ALWAYS WILL."

With a HUFF and a PUFF
and a miserable FROWN
he trekked off through the rain
to the far side of town…

...and beyond
through the valley
and over the sea

to a place
HIGH and LONELY
where no-one
would be.

"Now THIS is my hill,"
said Billy McGill.
"I live on my own!
Always have, always will."

The evening grew cold,
and as the sun set,
he thought of

the tiger,
the sheep,
and the vet,

and the dog,
and the bear,
and the
hairdresser too,

and just then
a red balloon
blew into view.

And the poor little baby
popped into his head,
the baby whose favourite
colour was red.

He reached for the string
and he went down the hill

and over the sea,
he kept going until

he had passed through the town
and arrived at his house.

The one with the dog
and the cat and the mouse.

There was noise and confusion
(and poop) EVERYWHERE
and the sheep was asleep
with the bear on the chair.

"I'll fix this!"
said Billy.

"I'll fix it
all soon!"

CHOO!

And he handed the baby
the bright red balloon.

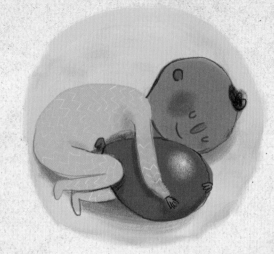

The baby stopped crying
and fell fast asleep

and the hairdresser
set about shearing the sheep.

The vet made
a sweater

the tiger soon wore.
And the tiger, much better, recovered its

ROAR!

The bear, in a panic,
ran out of the house
chasing after the dog
and the cat and the mouse.

The rest of them left
in a minute or so,
and Billy was pleased
to see everyone go.

"This is my hill," said Billy McGill.
"I live here alone!
Always have, always will."

Now Billy is happy,
and peace is restored.
His house on the hill
is in chaos no more!

There's hardly
a whisper.
There's barely
a sound!

Except on a
Tuesday...

...when friends
come around.

# The End